WHEN LOVE BECOMES AN OBSESSION

HARSH PARMAR

ISBN 979-888591529-8

Contents

Acknowledgements

Hi!

Thank you to all my readers who gave some of their precious time to read this book.

This book is not an effort of one person alone. First of all, I would like to thank my parents who gave their support and encouraged me for writing.

Then I would I like to offer my thanks to my friends for their invaluable support and time that they have given for the completion of this book.

I am also thankful to the team of Notion Press that gave me the opportunity to publish my work so that it can reach to millions of readers around the globe.

Last but not least, I once again thank my readers who chose my book over the others and found some time out of their schedule to read this book.

WHEN LOVE BECOMES AN OBSESSION

ONE

It was a usual morning but something was different for Harshit. It was his first day of college. Harshit Rajwansh, a 17-year boy, belonged to a middle-class family from a small town in Rajasthan. He was very simple, average looking and innocent. From his very childhood, he has been a bright student. It was his first day in college after he completed his high school. He was very excited and also nervous. With a smile on his face, he left for college.

The college campus was very vast. There were separate buildings for official work and each of the faculties. The campus also had canteen where several freshers were enjoying. Harshit was very happy to see everything and everyone. As he was the only one here from his old school, he had no friends yet. Harshit took a tour of the campus. Then, he enquired about his classes at the enquiry office and went up the stairs to his classroom. It was on the first floor. There were about fifty students in the class. Harshit greeted a hello to everyone and went towards his seat. The Professor entered the class and welcomed everyone. Students thanked him in response. He gave his introduction and briefed students about the curriculum and the subject he was going to teach.

The Professor started the class with a general question related to the subject. A girl answered the question. Her name was Aarohi Sharma. She was the daughter of a rich businessman in that town. The whole class turned to look at her. She was very beautiful. Harshit also looked at her and felt something for her. But he had low self-esteem in such matters. So, he instantly resisted this feeling thinking that he is not so worthy for her. And he immediately turned his attention to Professor.

TWO

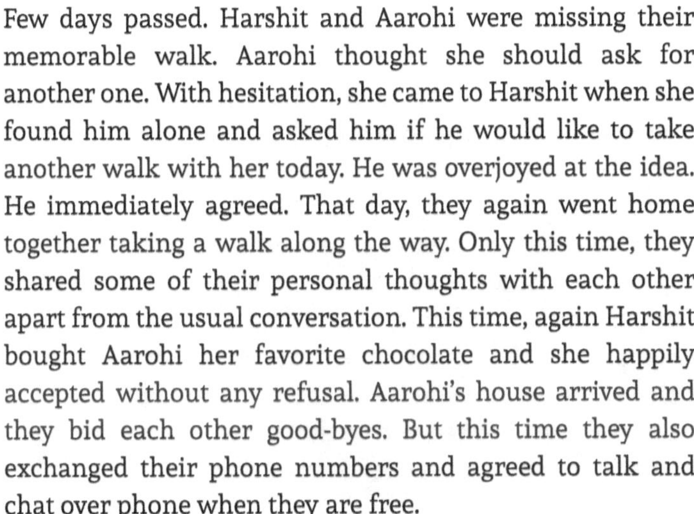

Few days passed. Harshit and Aarohi were missing their memorable walk. Aarohi thought she should ask for another one. With hesitation, she came to Harshit when she found him alone and asked him if he would like to take another walk with her today. He was overjoyed at the idea. He immediately agreed. That day, they again went home together taking a walk along the way. Only this time, they shared some of their personal thoughts with each other apart from the usual conversation. This time, again Harshit bought Aarohi her favorite chocolate and she happily accepted without any refusal. Aarohi's house arrived and they bid each other good-byes. But this time they also exchanged their phone numbers and agreed to talk and chat over phone when they are free.

That night, when Harshit was tucked in his bed, his phone beeped and screen flashed. It showed a message from Aarohi.

"Hi!" Aarohi had sent.

"Hello!" Harshit replied.

"Aren't you asleep? It's too late." Aarohi asked.

"No. Just finished today's homework." Harshit reasoned.

"Homework!!! Ooh! I completely forgot about it all in today's excitement."

"Don't worry dear. You still have tomorrow to complete it."

"Ah, yes. Thank God. Otherwise, I was going to get scolded tomorrow." Aarohi felt relaxed.

"Ok. Now go to sleep. I am feeling sleepy. Good night." Harshit said.

"Thank you for today's company and of course chocolate. Good night. Bye." Aarohi thanked.

"Welcome." Harshit replied and kept his phone aside to sleep.

Next day, they again went home together. Over the next few days, Harshit and Aarohi started going home together and chatted over phone more often. Gradually, they both grew fond of each other and started seeking each other's company. They started spending more time together. Even in college, they studied together, sat together in class, ate together in canteen and played and enjoyed in the college garden together. At home, they started chatting and talking over phone calls all the time. After reaching home from college, they both would wait for one another's call daily. They became obsessed and couldn't live without talking or chatting over phone even for a single day.

*

Harshit and Aarohi didn't know what was happening to them. They had never felt this way. They had never been this close to someone before. But, they thought, they would only be best friends and nothing else. However, life had other plans for them. Sometimes, Aarohi said they should stop talking to each other this much as this may end disastrous. But, Harshit kept on insisting her that it's just friendship and he likes talking to her and can't stop it. Aarohi trusted him more than she trusted herself. So, she simply agreed with him and didn't stop. They started talking about their parents, their life, their dreams. They also started sharing their personal feelings and thoughts with each other and also talked about the teen stuff sometimes. Every single moment of one's life was known to the other. Whatever happened in Aarohi's life, she merrily shared it with Harshit. Aarohi waited whole day sometimes to share her day with him. Harshit also shared his moments of happiness and sadness with her. They both were happy to find someone whom they can open their hearts to. Harshit's parents suspected that there is something going on with their son. That he is misleading. But they had their trust on him. So, they didn't tell him anything or stop him considering his age as this is the phase of life in which a person may become aggressive if his or her personal life is interfered.

Eventually, Harshit and Aarohi started getting closer and this attachment took a deep place in their hearts. They even set nicknames for each other. Aarohi would call Harshit as 'Harshi' and Harshit would call her 'Aru'. He started to admire and embrace her childish behavior. He loved her sweet voice and cute way of talking like a small child. As their bond grew stronger, they started talking over phone calls for late at nights that would rarely end before early morning. They kept talking even after wishing each other 'good night' for several times. They started sleeping together on phone calls daily. None of them could fall asleep without listening to each other's voice.

THREE

Days passed on. They started to care for one another with whole of their heart. Aarohi would cry in front of Harshit when she was sad and he would console her that all of bad times will end soon. He told her to pay no attention to her bad days and just be happy with what life offers.

Aarohi started developing feelings for Harshit. But she ignored these feelings worrying what would he think of her if he comes to know about this. With time, they both fell in love with each other without even realizing it. But both were afraid to admit and confess.

*

One night, they were chatting on phone.
"Hey, what are you doing sleepy head." Aarohi teased.
"Thinking about you." Harshit responded.
"Aww. My cute Harshi. Don't think too much about me."
"Well, I can't help it. After all, you are so nice."
Aarohi sent a flying kiss emoji.
The emoji was enough to make Harshit's feelings slip from his heart. He finally ended up confessing, "I love you, Aarohi."

Aarohi was surprised for a moment when she came to know that he also felt the same way as she did for him. She thought for a second but then responded with, "I love you too, Harshit."

With that, they began their journey towards an unintentional, unconditional and pure relationship. They had never expected or assumed themselves to be lovers. They always thought that their bond will always be confined to friendship. They were amused to see how their friendship changed to attachment, attachment into care and eventually care changed to love.

Until now, they had heard a common saying that sharing food and eating together brings you closer to one another. They thought it to be a myth. But, now, they realized that those people who said this really meant what they had said. They both shared food and ate together at the college canteen since the time they started hanging out and spending time together. Perhaps, it was what that brought them this close and made them fall in love.

Since then, their life began a new phase. It was pure, pleasant and a beautiful one indeed. It was of 'Love' – the most sacred of all the emotions that anyone could ever have.

*

Their relationship wasn't a show off. They acted like friends in public and shared their love in private. They became emotionally connected to one another. If one was happy, the other would smile and if one was sad, the other would also cry. Both were incomplete without each other.

Everything was going on well. They both trusted each other, respected each other and supported each other in every situation. Harshit sometimes felt insecure that he is not worthy enough for Aarohi. But, like any other girl in love, she was always by his side to pull him out of his insecurity. She was always there for Harshit whenever he needed her. They started getting serious for each other. They started imagining their future together. Whenever, they would talk, it was always about how their future would be like and their plans for the same. How they will continue their relationship, how they will live without seeing each other after college and where they will go in pursuit of career were few of the many things they always kept worrying about. They even started thinking about their wedding. They made plans of their own house, having two cute little kids- a boy and a girl, cooking together, talking for hours holding hands of each other, hugging and kissing each other every now and then, cuddling in their cozy bed, crying on each other's lap, having romantic fights and embrace and enjoy every moment of happiness and sadness together. In fact, they had no control over their thoughts. Their first love had made them fly so high that they forgot about stepping on ground.

Aarohi was a pampered child since her childhood. Her father fulfilled every demand she made. She was never kept devoid of anything. Everything was just a call away from her. But her parents were also quite conservative. She knew, they would never agree for love marriage of her daughter. They will never allow her to tie a knot with a boy of her own choice. Both of them respected their parents, so, none of them would leave them for their love. However, still considering all the worst situations along the path and the efforts and sacrifices they will have to make, they decided to do their best to convince their parents. No matter what the situations offer, they will always be by each other's side and will never break apart. They will always help each other, love each other and promised to be together forever.

They felt fortunate to have found each other. They spent most of their time together. Eating together, taking walks to home together, dreaming of future with each other, surprising each other at times with chocolates, supporting one another in every situation was all they ever wanted and that made them feel happy.

FOUR

Aarohi's birthday was in a few days. So Harshit started to plan a big surprise for her. On the day of her birthday, Harshit told one of Aarohi's friend to call her home. Harshit, his friends and Aarohi's friends had been there since morning for preparation and celebration of Aarohi's birthday. They had decorated the room with red and white balloons, colorful ribbons and 'HAPPY BIRTHDAY' balloons. They had also prepared a birthday cake all by themselves. In the evening, Aarohi arrived at her friend's place. Just as she entered, everyone wished her 'HAPPY BIRTHDAY' in chorus. She was surprised to find everyone there. She smiled and laughed with joy seeing the surprise. Then, she blew off the candle and cut the cake. Everyone grabbed the cake and put it on Aarohi's face. Her whole face got covered in cream. She looked no less than Santa Claus. After the cake war, everyone danced to various songs and had dinner together. After that, everyone left. They enjoyed the party very much and thanked Harshit for planning such a wonderful surprise. Aarohi, as usual, went home with Harshit. On the way, when the road was quiet and empty, Harshit stopped. He wished her happy birthday again and pulled out the gift from his pocket that he had bought for Aarohi. He gave it to her. When she opened it, her eyes got filled with tears of joy. It was a gold pendant having 'HA' engraved with platinum inside a heart. He tied the pendant around her neck but she removed it to keep her relationship secret from her parents. He kissed her forehead when Aarohi reached her home and left for his home. Aarohi had never received such a wonderful surprise before. She felt blessed today. She thanked God for giving her such lovely friends and a more loving boyfriend.

*

On a Sunday evening, Harshit and Aarohi went for a romantic movie that was recently released. They booked a corner seat to avoid any kind of prying eyes on them. While watching the movie, they fell in their dream world and started imagining themselves as movie characters. Aarohi watched the whole movie resting her head on Harshit's shoulder. And Harshit wrapped his arm around her. After the movie was over, Harshit took her for a walk in the city park. The park was full of crowd. There were families, children, couples and groups of friends enjoying the evening. The park illuminated in the lights. There was a fountain that was the real attraction. With some difficulty, Harshit and Aarohi managed to find an empty spot. He held her hands and they kept looking in each other's eyes without caring about anything and anyone. They were lost in the euphoric atmosphere of that evening. He moved his head close to Aarohi's, their eyes closed and their lips touched. She went back for a second but kissed him back. The world around them seemed to fall silent. It was their first kiss and an intense and passionate one. It felt so serene and magical that no one will ever forget. They hugged and embraced this special moment. But their silence was broken with the ringing of Aarohi's phone. Damn phone, she thought. It was a call from her mother asking her whereabouts. She lied that she is at her friend's place busy with studies and will be leaving in about an hour.

Next day, in college Aarohi was feeling ashamed to see Harshit. So, she ignored him all day. While leaving for home, Harshit caught her and enquired about the reason of her ignorance. She told him that it was about the kiss. She thought, it was too early for such physical connections. Harshit convinced her that it wasn't her fault. It was due to the hangover of the romantic movie they watched or probably the euphoric evening was responsible. Though whatever be the reason, it felt splendid and magical and that's what made yesterday's evening memorable for them. Aarohi kissed her again and smiled biting her lips. Seeing her smile, Harshit also smiled.

*

It was about time for the winter to end and a college trip was planned by the college officials. The trip was to Shimla. It was a 5-days trip. The travel cost was provided by the college but students had to make their own arrangements for lodging and fooding. Harshit and Aarohi both were ready to go. How could they miss the most awaited chance for being together, away from their parents, after all? As they had to make their own lodging arrangements, they booked a hotel room for just themselves for the entire trip duration. Now they can spend every moment of each day by each other's side without worrying to hide from anyone for a few days at least.

The trip was such a blast. The hill station at the end of winter was no less than a paradise. The streets were covered with patches of white snow all around. Trees, house tops and roofs were covered with snow. On the first day of the trip, they visited Jakhu Temple. It is an ancient temple dedicated to Lord Hanuman. The temple is home to a tall statue of Lord Hanuman. Being situated at the top of Jakhu

Hill, the way to the temple offers a scenic view of the nature around. There was some un-melted snow on the way. View from the top of the hill is panoramic and sublime. The environment of the temple was so quiet and divine that any devotee wouldn't want to leave.

On the second day, they visited The Mall Road. Situated in the heart of the city, it offers a major source of tourist attraction. It houses several dining restaurants, clubs and local handicraft market. It is also home to Kali Bari Temple and Gaiety Theatre. Couples, families, tourists and locals enjoy and spend some quality time together in the evening. The students had a fine lunch at one of the restaurants after visiting the temple there. In the evening, they gathered at Gaiety Theatre to watch a cultural performance.

On the third day, visit to The Ridge was planned. It is a hub to various cultural activities. There, they visited Christ Church. There were statues of some personalities near the road. After enjoying the attractions here, everyone headed to Lakkar Bazar, a wooden crafts market. There were so many eye-catching crafts and sculptures made out of wood. A showpiece in which a boy was proposing to a girl with a ring in his hand caught Aarohi's attention. She started pleading Harshit to buy her the showpiece. At first, Harshit didn't agree but when she kept on insisting, he bought her that showpiece. She kissed him when she got the lovely woodwork.

On the fourth day, they had to visit Chadwick Falls. It is a great destination for all the nature lovers. The place offers serenity, dense forests and tranquil atmosphere. Being so near to the nature, the child inside Aarohi woke up. She jumped in the water taking Harshit along with her. Seeing them, several of their fellow classmates also took a dive. They got fully wet. Harshit and Aarohi had a water fight.

Their whole day was spent enjoying in the water. They didn't get out until they started to shiver from cold. The day near the nature, away from the hustle and bustle of the city was much needed for everyone to admire the beauty of nature.

It was the fifth day. It was meant to be the last day of the trip. It had to be a special and memorable one. It was planned that they would visit Kufri Fun World, an amusement park in Kufri near Shimla. It offers various sources of entertainment such as Go Karting, High Rope Course, Giant Wheel, Swing Chairs and many more. It also harbors an Apple Orchard. Harshit and Aarohi took the Giant Wheel ride first. The view of the place from the top of the wheel was magnificent. After the ride, they experienced the thrill of High Rope Course. One by one, they visited every ride. Before leaving, everyone visited the Apple Orchard to pluck some apples to take with them. The apples were sweet though.

As they had to leave for home the next day, after returning from the amusement park, Harshit and Aarohi began packing their stuff together. After they were done, they ordered dinner and fed each other. This trip had brought them much close. Their relationship became more compassionate and intimate. Every night, they slept after talking to each other for hours and cuddled in one another's arm. Just when Aarohi was going to bed, Harshit caught her by her hand. He wanted to feel her one last time before they leave. He kissed her passionately. His fingers crawled down her waist. He felt the urge to undo her clothes. But he pushed himself back thinking that it was too early to make love. Aarohi kissed him again and they felt each other one last time.

*

Next morning, they had to leave early for their return. Everyone gathered at the location decided and boarded the bus. Along the way, everyone started recalling the fun they had during the trip. Harshit and Aarohi took the back seat. They were sitting holding each other's hand and Aarohi had her head rest on Harshit's shoulder. They were watching the trees passing by and embracing and admiring their love.

Finally, they came back home. They told their parents how much fun they had there, what places they visited, what delicacies they tasted and everything else, but, skipping their private moments. It was an unforgettable trip for both of them. They never wanted this trip to end.

FIVE

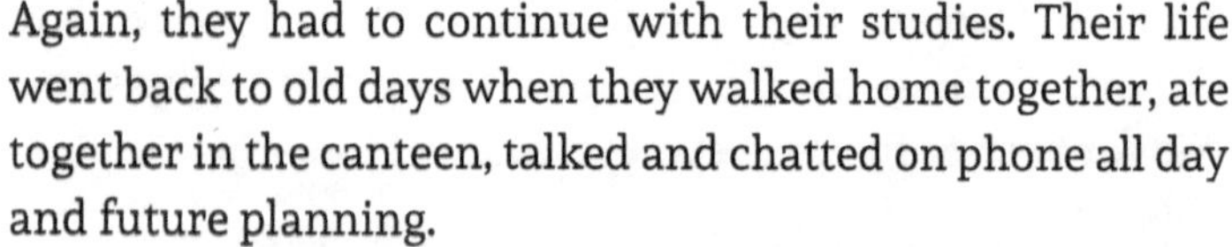

Again, they had to continue with their studies. Their life went back to old days when they walked home together, ate together in the canteen, talked and chatted on phone all day and future planning.

Dreams of being together were working well. But, as they say, good things don't last long and they eventually come to an end. Same happened with Harshit and Aarohi. Within a month of their relationship, something happened that turned their world upside down. Aarohi's father was always suspicious of her change in behavior. So, one day, when she wasn't around, her father checked her phone. What he found made him furious with rage. His face turned red in anger. He immediately summoned Aarohi and her mother. He showed her mother what was on her phone. Her mother was awestruck finding what her daughter was up to. There were romantic messages, I Love Yous', heart and kiss emojis, pictures of her with Harshit, etc. Her parents demanded explanation. She was afraid what will happen now but somehow, mustering up some courage she told them that they love each other and want to build their future together. This was enough to set her parents' conservative thoughts on fire. Her father slapped her hard for the first time in her life. He threatened her that if he ever finds out they are still together, he will get Harshit killed.

Aarohi couldn't say a word. She kept on weeping until her eyes ran out of tears.

That night, when Harshit called, Aarohi told him everything that had happened and started crying. He went numb knowing that the first love of his life is going away from him. He didn't know what to say or what to do. He was just afraid that he would lose her forever. Harshit didn't want Aarohi to go against her parents' will after everything that had happened. He consoled Aarohi.

"Don't cry Aru. Perhaps destiny never wanted to see us together." Harshit tried to stop her crying.

"You don't know Harshit how deeply I am attached to you and how much I love you."

"I understand sweetheart. I also love you so much that it's hard to explain in words."

"Then why do we need to separate? Why my parents don't want to see their daughter happy for once in her life."

"Calm down, Aru. Maybe I was not the right choice. You will find someone much better than me."

"I don't want to find anyone else. I want you and only you."

"Don't worry. I will always be there for you. We can still remain friends just like before."

"Go, get some sleep Harshit."

"Only when you stop crying."

"I am not crying." Aarohi said wiping her tears.

"That's better. Let's talk tomorrow. Good night."

"Good night."

"If I were there, I would have hugged you tight and kissed till your lips became dry." Harshit tried to make her smile.

"Shut up and go to sleep." Aarohi said smiling.

*

Next day, they skipped their classes. They went to the city park where they can find some personal space to sort things out. They found the exact same spot where they had witnessed their first kiss. They cried there with whole of their heart with Aarohi resting her head on Harshit's lap. Then, Harshit held her hand, looked in her eyes and said, "I will always love you and be there for you. But I don't want things to get worse. So, from now on, we will be best friends, no hard feelings."

Aarohi wanted to deny but she reluctantly agreed. She had no choice. She didn't want Harshit to land in trouble because of her.

Sadly, the typical conservative mindset got in the way of a precious relationship which became the cause of separation of two souls who were meant for each other. And a pure, undemanding and unexpected relationship met its tragic end.

SIX

After the incident with Aarohi's father and separation between Aarohi and Harshit, they both stopped talking to each other for several days. They even stopped making eye contact and started to ignore each other totally. They thought that staying away from one another can help them heal their pain. But things didn't work out as they thought. Flashes of memories kept playing in Harshit's mind. He recalled how he admired her, fed her with his own hand, his first kiss, walking down the street holding her hand, hugging her to stop her cry, etc. Meanwhile, things weren't going well with Aarohi too. She used to keep herself locked in her room only to come out when called to have some food. She kept crying all day thinking about him, his childish behavior, his possessive attitude for her, his care for her, how he always supported her, how they used to talk all day and night, etc. Their feelings started to overwhelm and they were growing desperate without each other.

When you love someone so deeply, your emotions and feelings take complete control over you. The more you resist and try to be away, the more it reminds you how adorable you looked together.

*

One day, when college canteen was quite empty, Aarohi came to Harshit and said that she needs to talk about something. They grabbed a corner table where they can hardly get noticed. She told him everything about how she was feeling for the past few days. Harshit told her that things aren't easy with him too. Tears rolled down their eyes but they tried to hide it and sobbed silently pretending to be okay. They realized that avoiding each other won't help. So, they shall start the conversation and spend some time together but less often and they will try to control every feeling and stay best friends as decided earlier.

So, their life turned to a new phase- Friendship. Now they started spending some time together and talking over phone. They walked to their homes together. But all this now had its limits set. They both tried to suppress each hard feeling to the best they could. Their day long phone calls were now limited to late night calls. Pain and sorrow they felt was known to both but they pretended to look cheerful in front of one another. Previously, on calls, they used to talk about their future together, their wishes which they want to fulfil with one another, their wedding, having kids and all. Now, the subject was changed to recalling the moments spent together which had now become nothing but memories. They would remember their night long talks, their hugs and kisses, taking care of each other, sharing food, surprising each other and how badly they wanted to be always together. They wondered why God has casted this curse on them. Why did they meet and fell in love in the first place, if destiny never wanted them to stay together? Sometimes, they wished, if life would have been a fairy tale and they had a magic wand, their every problem would be just a flick away from solution.

But unwantedly, Harshit and Aarohi had to face reality out of their fancy thoughts. Sometimes, while recalling everything, one of them would sob silently, but the other always sensed it and they both ended up crying and falling asleep in tears. Now, most of their mornings started with each other's thoughts and dreams and nights ended with recalling memories and crying.

Harshit and Aarohi got used to talking again but not too much. This helped them heal their wounds to some extent but the scars will prevail forever. Love was so intense between them that sometimes while talking, their feelings would slip from their hearts and they spilled all the romantic stuff like I love you, please be with me forever, don't go leaving me alone, I am so lonely without you or whatever one felt about the other.

SEVEN

One Sunday, they wanted to meet each other. So, they went to the city park. Both of them had to lie to their parents that they are going to a friend's place to study and had to carry their bags. They greeted each other with a handshake at the park entrance and went in to find a quiet place. Now, their meetings were limited to a handshake unlike before, when they used to hug and kiss whenever they met. They talked for a while. Suddenly, Aarohi remembered something.

"Oops, I forgot, I brought something for you." Aarohi said reminding.

"Wait, let me take it out." said Aarohi.

While searching through the bag, Aarohi's fingers fiddled upon something. She took it out only to find that it was the gold pendant that Harshit had gifted her.

"You remember this, Harshit?" Aarohi asked.

"Of course. How can I forget? I gave it to you on your birthday." said Harshit.

"You know what, I always wished to wear it after our marriage when no one would question about it." Aarohi confessed.

Her eyes turned moist and tears escaped her eyes. Harshit calmed her down.

"Sorry, here, take this. I searched four shops to find it." Aarohi gave him what she had brought after wiping her tears.

It was a packet of 'Ferrero Rocher', Harshit's favorite chocolate. They both shared a bite of Ferrero Rocher balls and headed back to home. On the way, they crossed a bridge over the river. Aarohi stopped on the bridge. She took out the pendant, wore and kissed it for one last time and threw it in the river. Harshit just saw her and felt sad that his only gift is now thrown to rot in the river water. Aarohi apologized for what she did and explained him that if she had kept the pendant, then it would have always reminded her that she cannot spend her life with him and this would make her sad than anything else. Harshit understood her grief but kept crying inside. Then, they went back home.

After reaching home, Aarohi burned all the pictures she had with Harshit. She deleted all the romantic chats between them. She even burned the showpiece Harshit had purchased for her in Shimla. She wanted to get rid of all the things that may remind her about that precious relationship.

EIGHT

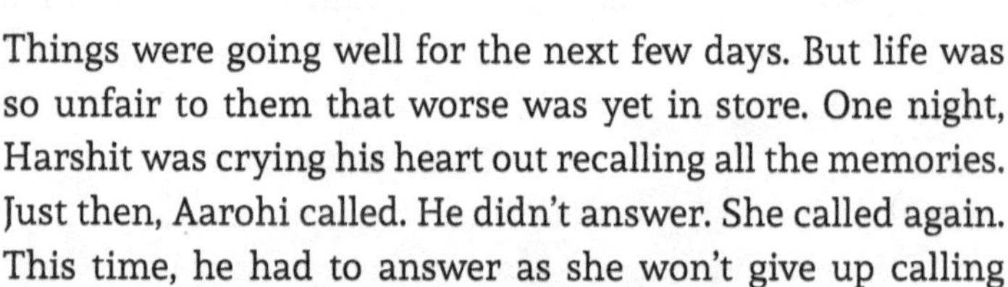

Things were going well for the next few days. But life was so unfair to them that worse was yet in store. One night, Harshit was crying his heart out recalling all the memories. Just then, Aarohi called. He didn't answer. She called again. This time, he had to answer as she won't give up calling until he picks up. He composed himself and picked up the call.

"Hey, were you asleep?"' asked Aarohi.

"No." Harshit replied.

Aarohi sensed from his voice that he was sad and crying.

"Why are you crying, Harshi?" Aarohi asked.

"No, I am not crying." Harshit denied.

"Yes, you are. Now tell me the reason behind your tears. You know, I can't see you crying."

"I was thinking about our moments together. I so deeply wanted to spend my life with you."

Aarohi got irritated with his sentence. In anger, she spilled out some words which she should never have. She shouted at him that he will always remain a child, immature, attention hungry, pervert, insecure and always lurking after girls. She also told him that he will always be devoid of true love and she no longer wants to talk to him. Her words acted like pointy needles and pierced Harshit's heart and he couldn't control his tears now. He loved and trusted her so much that he couldn't speak a word. Instead, he just listened silently. He convinced himself, "Aarohi doesn't mean these words. It's her anger talking. Everything will be alright in the morning." But he was unaware of the fact that these words will plant a seed of hatred and distrust in his heart that will make him lose his friendship with Aarohi and he will gradually step on the wrong track.

Next morning, Harshit texted Aarohi apologizing for the last night. But she didn't respond. He called her. She picked up but didn't talk in her usual tone. She was still angry with him. Harshit tried to fix things but she just wasn't ready. She begged him to leave her alone and to never call or text her again. She doesn't want to be with him anymore. Harshit kept on requesting her to calm down but she hung up. Now, Harshit started losing faith on Aarohi. He started to think that there is no such thing as 'True Love'. It is just a fantasy of human mind. Still, he tried his best to get her back. From calls to texts, apologizing to begging, he tried everything. But she started avoiding him completely as if nothing had happened between them. She started to see him as a stranger.

*

Now, the worst was about to come. Harshit was completely broken and lost. Words like attachment, care, love and trust now meant nothing to him. He swore to himself that he will never fall in love again. He wanted to forget everything. He tried to find escape from the grief and loss. He started hanging out with friends. His friends were a real deal. At first, they forced him to smoke and then abused him with alcohol, telling him that it will help him forget her. However, nothing helped. Aarohi's words kept playing in his mind on repeat. He lost his sleep, appetite and his class performance started to deteriorate. His mind which once saw good in everything and love everywhere, now, thought of nothing but hatred and evil.

NINE

One night, Harshit was tossing and turning in bed, trying to sleep. Suddenly, an idea popped up in his evil mind to kill Aarohi's father. He tried to suppress this idea. He tried everything from ignoring her to deleting all her pictures to deleting all the chats to finally become an alcohol addict. But nothing helped him out of his misery. Day by day, the idea started to dig its root deep in his mind and he started thinking and planning over it. His mind used to say, "If you can't get the girl, kill her father for vengeance." And Harshit, though knowing it is wrong, couldn't restrain from the fact that her father was the reason behind his relationship's miserable end.

Days passed and this evil desire started to demand the execution. Harshit came up with a plan. He hired some men to kidnap Aarohi's father and briefed them with his plan. Now, his plan was ready to be executed.

Harshit purchased a new mobile number. He called Aarohi's father with that number and lured him in the name of his daughter. He lied that his daughter is lying unconscious on a highway just outside the city. Please come and get her to a hospital. It's an emergency. Now, like any other parent, Aarohi's father got anxious and fell for the trap. When he reached the location, he found that he is fooled. There, Harshit's hired men were waiting for Aarohi's father. They kidnapped him and brought him to an abandoned warehouse outside the city. Harshit was waiting there sipping whiskey. He paid his men off and turned to Aarohi's father.

"You?" Aarohi's father glanced with anger.

"Yes. Me." Harshit laughed.

"It's good that my daughter left you. You are such a drunkard."

"Probably, yes. Now, your daughter will lose her father."

Harshit slapped him and said, "This is the reward for hitting my girl."

He slapped him again and said, "This one is for threatening her to kill me."

"What do you think? You will kill me and get on unnoticed?" Aarohi's father threatened him.

"You don't need to worry about me. Now say your last prayers."

He tied him to a pole with a thick rope.

"Free me or else you will pay for this." Aarohi's father warned him.

"There is no one here to save you. Who will make me pay? Now shut your damn mouth."

"Harm me and you will see."

Harshit took out a knife from his pocket and cut Aarohi's father's both wrists.

"Now I will bleed you dry." Harshit laughed.

Harshit was enjoying sitting and watching his plan work. Just then, he heard police car's siren. He got alert and confused at the same time that how did the police came to know about him. He ran to escape. But as he reached the gate, the police caught him. Now, Aarohi's father was laughing at Harshit. The police untied the victim and provided him first aid. Aarohi's father came close to Harshit and said, "See, I told you. Now you will pay for your deed and rot in jail."

Harshit was surprised how his masterplan could fail. Aarohi's father couldn't leave him in suspense. He revealed everything to Harshit. It turns out that, since the day Aarohi's father came to know about his daughter's love affair, he hired a man to keep an eye on both, Harshit and Aarohi. He paid him for it and he was instructed to inform the police if anything goes wrong. The man hired by Aarohi's father was one among those hired by Harshit. So, as soon as he was paid by Harshit, he went to the police station and filed an FIR against Harshit. The police immediately took charge and arrested Harshit. They took him to the police custody and tortured him. Aarohi's father was sent to home safely in one of the police cars.

*

In the custody, the police beat and tortured Harshit until he spilled everything about his life, his affair and his so-called masterplan. His parents were called to the police station. They broke down in tears seeing their son in blood and pain. The inspector in-charge filled Harshit's parents with his intentions. They were shocked hearing all that. They couldn't believe the fact that their once innocent and generous son would do something like this for a girl. They felt the ground beneath their feet moving. They went towards Harshit. He couldn't look into his parents' eyes. How could he, after what he had done? His father couldn't bear the shame and slapped him. The inspector told them that his act is a criminal offense and requires a judicial trial which is on next Wednesday. Till then, he will have to stay here. Then, Harshit's parents left.

When they reached home, they were bombarded with questions from neighbors and relatives. Harshit was all over the news by that time. They didn't respond to any of those questions and went inside the house.

Till now, Aarohi had no idea about all this. Even her father didn't tell her the truth that his ex-boyfriend attempted to murder him. When she watched the news, she couldn't stop the tears coming out of her eyes. She buried her face in her mother's lap and cried. She started to tell that it was all her fault. If she hadn't been so cruel to him that day, all this would have never happened. Her mother consoled her and told her, "This boy was never good. He had started smoking and drinking after you two broke-up. It's good that your father had his back-up and Harshit got arrested. Otherwise, you would have lost your father and I would have lost my husband today."

*

On the day of court's session, Harshit arrived directly to court from the police custody. He attempted to flee while coming out of the police car, but failed at his attempt. He was handcuffed and led to the hearing room. Harshit's parents were in tears. It was the worst day of their life, seeing their son in court for the accusation of attempt to murder. Aarohi was sitting with her parents on the front bench. Harshit couldn't meet her eyes.

The Judge entered and the session began. Harshit was charged for kidnapping and an attempt to murder. He admitted his crime. He was sentenced six years of imprisonment on the charge of attempt to murder.

After the court was dismissed, Harshit came out of the court handcuffed with two police constables. When he was about to enter the police car, Aarohi called him and he stopped. His parents, Aarohi's parents and Aarohi came up to him. Aarohi didn't say a word. She just glared at Harshit with eyes full of hatred and guilt. Hatred because he tried to kill her father and guilt because somewhere it was her fault that he had to take this step in his agony and solitude. Her parents also didn't say anything. Harshit's parents hugged him for the last time. They apologized to Aarohi's parents for their son's wrong deeds. But Aarohi's mother stopped them and convinced them that it wasn't their fault but they shouldn't have let Harshit so much free. Seeing his parents apologize for his crime, brought tears in his eyes. But what could he do? It was after all his evil mind that brought this day to everyone's life. The constables then put Harshit in the car and led on their way to city jail.

TEN

Worst days began for Harshit and his family. In jail, Harshit had to live with minimum requirements. He had to do labor. He was given meal twice a day which was too simple to eat for any person. Meanwhile, his parents were always bombarded with taunts and comments from neighbors and relatives. They had to spend the day listening to everything others had to say and slept at night with a stone on their hearts. They always cried for their son. At times, they used to visit him but how could they be at peace while their son is suffering in jail.

Things weren't at ease with Aarohi also. Her parents didn't want any more of boyfriend-girlfriend drama, so they had started planning her marriage. They started finding a suitable boy for her. Her family and relatives, everyone lend their hand in finding a perfect match for her, so that, as soon as they find one, Aarohi shall marry him and move on from the tragedy that had fallen upon her. Aarohi wasn't ready to marry but she knew that her parents won't stop. So, she couldn't refuse.

Finally, Aarohi's parents found a match for her. The groom-to-be was the CEO of 'TECH HELP', an IT consultancy agency in Delhi. His name was Akshit. He was quite rich and soft-spoken. Both families met and fixed a date for marriage ceremony. Wedding invitation cards were printed and distributed. Wedding shopping had begun. Saree, wedding ring, necklace, bangles, ear rings, other jewelry, shoes and many other things were selected for Aarohi.

When Aarohi found some time out of this wedding preparations, she took a wedding card and went out to visit Harshit in city jail. Seeing Aarohi after so long, brought tears in Harshit's eyes. Aarohi's eyes also turned moist but she controlled herself. Harshit started apologizing to her for all that he had done. But she stopped him, gave him the wedding card and said, "Take it. It's because of you that I have to marry so soon. Now all my dreams are crushed. I am as good as dead. You are invited to see me crying for the last time. I hope this will make you happy and you will show up. Rot here now. Bye."

Then Aarohi left suppressing her tears. Harshit left crying out loud holding the wedding card where he once wished to see his name beside Aarohi's. But fate was not so kind to him and now she is gone forever.

*

The day of the wedding arrived. Families and relatives gathered at the wedding venue. Groom was wearing a white sherwani, embroidered and laced with gold. Bride was wearing a red saree. They sat beside the sacred fire and the priest started the rituals.

Suddenly, out of nowhere, a loud voice said, "Stop the wedding." Everyone was taken aback by the voice. Then, Harshit showed up with a knife in his hand and looking towards Aarohi he said, "See Aarohi. I actually showed up." He broke the prison. He threatened to kill himself if the wedding rituals proceed any further. The priest paused. Meanwhile, Aarohi's father called police silently. Just when, Harshit was trying to steal Aarohi from the wedding, police came and arrested him once again. He was again taken to jail. He was kept in a cell with a 24-hour check on him. The wedding continued. After seven rounds around the sacred fire, Akshit and Aarohi were declared officially married.

Then, there were post-marriage rituals and Aarohi bid her family farewell and went with Akshit to her in- laws home.

*

Harshit's life was nothing but miserable in jail. After he broke the prison, he was not allowed to meet anyone. He was given work all day which if he didn't complete, he was beaten. He lived his life in solitude and guilt. Sometimes, the memories brought smile on his face, but, most of the time, he kept crying about his crime. After what he did, no one will ever forgive him.

Aarohi gave up her every dream to make her marriage work. Her in-laws were very supportive and treated her as their own daughter. She was happy to find such a home. After about a year of her marriage, Aarohi gave birth to a boy. She took great care of him and also looked after the family.

Her son grew older. One day, he found a picture of his mom with Harshit in Aarohi's belongings. He showed it to Aarohi and asked, "Mommy, who is this guy sitting beside you holding your hand?"

Aarohi didn't know how this picture was left with her after everything she had burned. She didn't say anything. She kept quiet. Her deep buried feelings resurfaced and flashes of memories played through her mind. She hugged her son tight and cried a lot until her eyes ran short of tears. Then, she composed herself and said, "He was a friend of mine." to her son. She burned the picture to destroy even the last bit of anything that will remind her of Harshit. Now, she has dedicated her life to her family and her son.

*